BALBOA.
PRESS
A DIVISION OF HAY HOUSE

This book is dedicated to Humanities Awakening.
Many thanks to The Rodan Foundation's loving community, as well as my family and friends...especially Naim,
Grandma Mae, and the Kenny/Flood family.
Your unconditional love fills me and inspires me to wake up!
Let's awaken together.
~Kristen Walton

This book is dedicated to my loving family for all
of their support and encouragement they
give me every day. I love you all, but
special thanks to
Richard, Tracy, Priscilla, Michelle, and Jacob Rodgers.
~Andrew Rodgers

Interior Art Credit: Andrew Rodgers

Balboa Press books may be ordered through booksellers or by contacting:

Balboa Press
A Division of Hay House
1663 Liberty Drive
Bloomington, IN 47403
www.balboapress.com
1 (877) 407-4847

Because of the dynamic nature of the Internet, any web addresses or links contained in this book may have changed since publication and may no longer be valid. The views expressed in this work are solely those of the author and do not necessarily reflect the views of the publisher, and the publisher hereby disclaims any responsibility for them.

This is a work of fiction. All of the characters, names, incidents, organizations, and dialogue in this novel are either the products of the author's imagination or are used fictitiously.

Any people depicted in stock imagery provided by Thinkstock are models, and such images are being used for illustrative purposes only.

Certain stock imagery © Thinkstock.

Library of Congress Control Number: 2017919600

ISBN: 978-1-5043-9436-9 (sc)
ISBN: 978-1-5043-9437-6 (e)

Print information available on the last page.

Balboa Press rev. date: 01/31/2018

Light
in the
Enchanted
Forest

by
Kristen Walton
Illustrated
by Andrew Rodgers

"Welcome to the Kingdom,"
said the Butterfly Queen and King.
"We gather here together
to celebrate and sing.

The Enchanted Forest is shifting,
and changing everyday
as we grow out of old behaviors,
and live in a new way."

"We are moving out of density,
connecting with our light,
trusting in our higher selves,
and giving up the fight."

"We must generate
Love, Trust, Forgiveness, and Gratitude
by changing our perspective
and our attitude.
You will notice some thoughts that you will need to
let go, practice acceptance,
and get in the flow!"

"Release
Fear, Judgement, and Resistance to Change.
At the beginning the adjustment
might feel a bit strange."

The insects looked
at each other,
"Simple!" they said.
All agreed to the intention
it is love they would spread.

The Bees began buzzing away, making their honey and working all day.

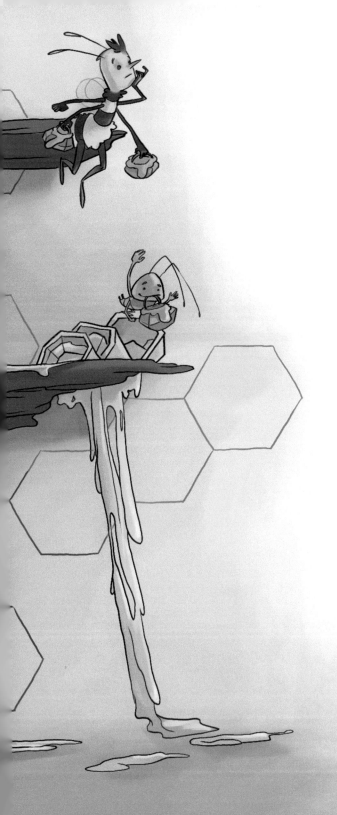

One Bee thought,
"This isn't
fair!
I am working much faster than
the bee over there!"

Then he remembered
what the Queen had said.
He released the judgement
out of his head.
"I choose to accept my fellow Bee.
We are all one, and I love thee."

With this forgiveness
the Bees were gifted,
with peace and love,
the darkness was lifted.

Close to the Bees
lived the laboring Ants,
marching along and
humming their chants.

The Ants were harvesting,
collecting their food,
working very hard,
and in a good mood.

The King flew by with an unusual request.
For the Ants to pave a trail
now facing

west.

"Instead of marching around the Great Rock,

go over,"

he said. The Ants were in shock!

"**WHAT?**"
said the Captain who
was the leader for many years.
"It's our tradition!"
and he
broke into tears.

"Remember,"
said the youngest Ant,
"to let resistance go,
change can be good,
and stay in the flow.
Let's try this new way
and see how we do,
trust in ourselves,
and support each other, too."

"Fantastic!"
said the Captain,
as he experienced success.
"This change is very fun,
and we are working less."

Positivity filled the hearts
of the Ant colony,
touching every creature,
and creating harmony.

Nearby the Ant hill
was an apple tree,
where a family of spiders
loved to be.

Baby Spider was sad and
feeling really down.
Not catching any food, and
wearing a big frown.

Grandmother Spider came over to him.
His energy was low, and he was looking grim.
"What is the matter precious spider of mine?
Go up by the Apples, the bugs are divine."

"What if a bird eats me today?
Just this morning I saw a hungry
Blue Jay!"

Grandmother Spider said,
"Have no fear!
Trust my
love,
my sweet dear.

Fear is an illusion,
and will keep us in a trap.
We are very powerful
and weave our own map.

Instead we trust,
and use our awareness.
We build strong webs
and refuse to be careless."

With gratitude for Grandmother Spider's advice, Baby Spider climbed up,

way up to new heights.

He caught many bugs and
was safe in the tree.
He realized that confidence
was his golden key.

The Queen and King admired
such a beautiful sight
as they flew over
the Enchanted Forest that night.

All of the Kingdom
was sparkling bright,
as everyone chose
to live their own light.

Love,
Trust,
Forgiveness,
and
Gratitude
creates a high vibration with
infinite magnitude!
"Blessings to All of YOU Beings of Light,
Live your life in love and you will shine
bright!"

Close your eyes and begin to
notice your breath..

Breathe in Light:
Breathe in Chi:
Life Force Energy

As you inhale,
Feel your entire body with Love
Imagine all of your cells
embraced in love

As you exhale,
Send this love vibration to
everyone you know..
The trees, animals, water,
friends, and family.
Anyone and everything...

As you continue to do this,
You will feel the love building in your heart.
Your body will fill with light.

You will feel a shift inside of you
as your spirit
begins to awaken.

Open the door to heart awareness.
Surprises are awaiting for you to enjoy!